Army Ants

Written by Carol Krueger

Look at these ants.
They are called army ants.
Army ants live in the jungle.
They live in a big family.

Army ants have eyes,
but they can't see very well.
They have feelers.
Their feelers show them
where to go.

feeler

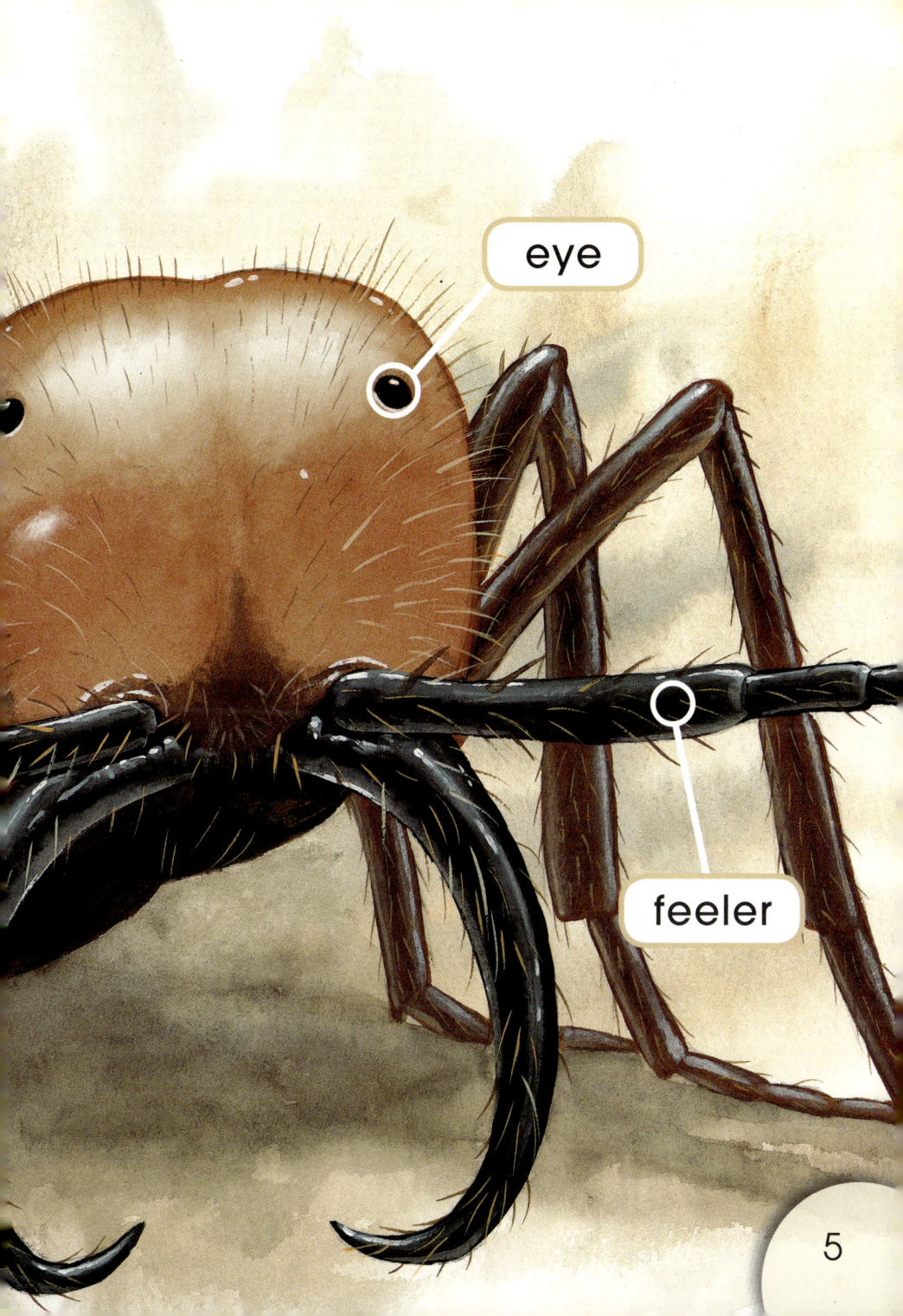

Army ants look for their food in the day.
They make a nest at night.
Lots and lots of army ants live in this nest.

There can be one million army ants in a nest!

Army ants don't make their nest with sticks and leaves. They make their nest out of ants! They hold on with their claws and jaws.

moth

Army ants get food with their claws and jaws, too.
They eat insects and lizards.
They could eat a pig, too!

Some ants get food to take back to the nest. They take care of the eggs, too.

Some ants in the nest are called worker ants.

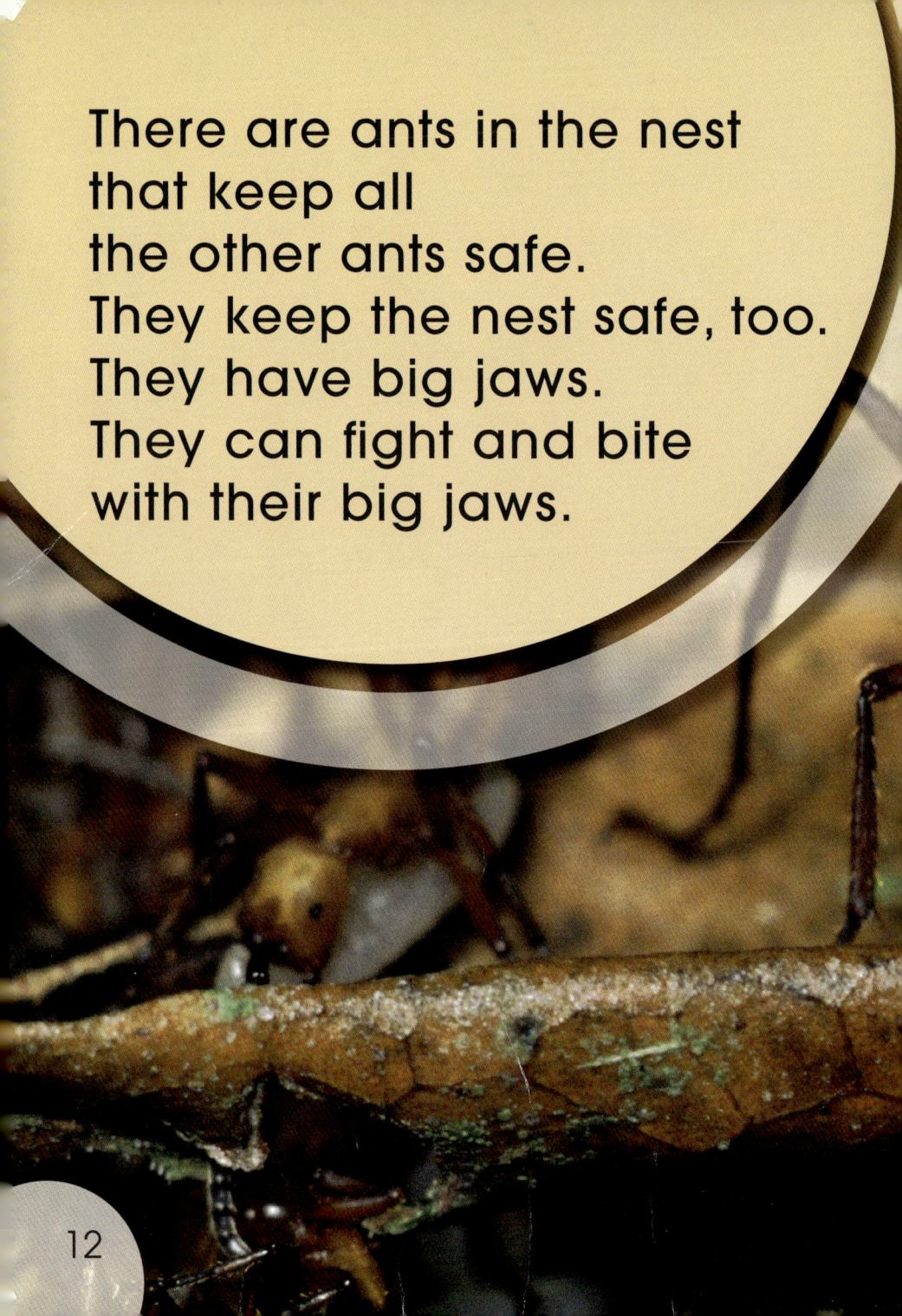

There are ants in the nest
that keep all
the other ants safe.
They keep the nest safe, too.
They have big jaws.
They can fight and bite
with their big jaws.

Some ants in the nest are called soldier ants.

jaws

The nest has a queen ant.
She is very big and lays all the eggs.
If the queen ant dies, all the army ants could die, too!

queen ant

Index

army ant
   claws 8-9
   eggs 10, 14
   eyes 4
   feelers 4
   food 6, 9, 10
   jaws 8-9, 12
   nests 6, 8, 10, 12

queen ant 14
where army ants
   live 2

eggs

Guide Notes

Title: Army Ants
Stage: Early (4) – Green

Genre: Nonfiction
Approach: Guided Reading
Processes: Thinking Critically, Exploring Language, Processing Information
Written and Visual Focus: Photographs (static images), Index, Labels, Captions, Illustrations
Word Count: 188

THINKING CRITICALLY
(sample questions)
- Look at the front cover and the title. Ask the children what they know about army ants.
- Look at the title and read it to the children.
- Focus the children's attention on the index. Ask: "What are you going to find out about in this book?"
- Ask the children what they know about how an army ant makes its nest.
- If you want to find out about how an army ant makes its nest, what pages would you look on?
- Look at pages 10 and 11. How do you think the army ants would carry a pig back to their nest?
- Look at pages 12 and 13. Why do you think a solider ant has such big jaws?

EXPLORING LANGUAGE

Terminology
Title, cover, photographs, author, photographers

Vocabulary
Interest words: army, jungle, feelers, nest, jaws, worker, soldier, queen
High-frequency words: called, could, show, keep
Positional words: in, on, out

Print Conventions
Capital letter for sentence beginnings, periods, commas, exclamation marks